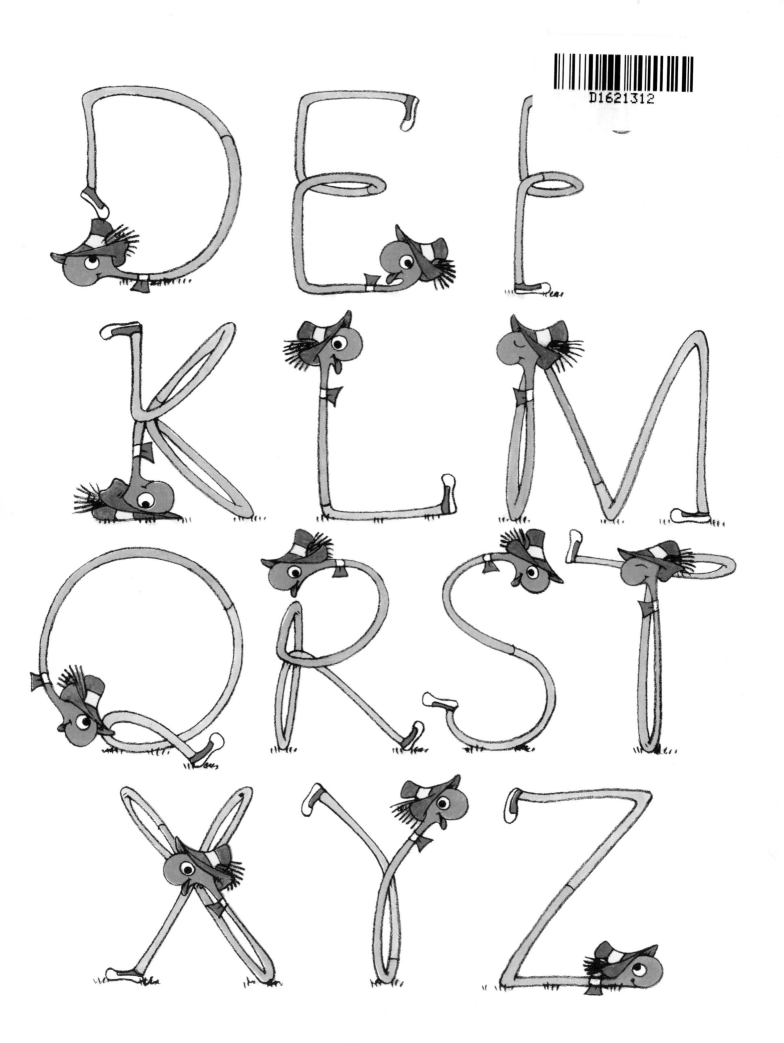

This book belongs to

....

....

First published in hardback in Great Britain by HarperCollins *Children's Books* in 2013.

HarperCollins *Children's Books* is a division of HarperCollins *Publishers* Ltd,
77-85 Fulham Palace Road, London W6 8JB.

1 3 5 7 9 10 8 6 4 2

ISBN: 978-0-00-752314-6

The HarperCollins website address is www.harpercollins.co.uk

Printed and bound in China.

Richard Scarry's

Best Lowly
Worm Book

Ever!

HarperCollins *Children's Books*

Lowly

Book

Richard Scarry's
Best
Worm
Ever!

Good Morning, Lowly!

I am a worm. My name is Lowly Worm.

I get up in the morning
and wash my face and foot.

It's a little bit difficult,
but I can dress myself.

Everyone helps to make breakfast at the Cat family house where I live.

After breakfast, Huckle, Sally and I clear the table.

Father Cat washes the dishes.

We make our beds.

Hey!
Where is Lowly?

We tidy our rooms and hang up our clothes.

Then we say goodbye to Mother Cat, and go to the school bus stop.

Off to School

We are careful crossing the road.
We look both ways.

We walk and do not run.

We say "Good morning" to
the school bus driver.

We sit quietly in our
seats on the way to
school. Arthur shows me
his new toy police car.

I bring an apple to Miss Honey, the schoolteacher.

Huckle draws a picture of me.

I help Sally to string beads.

I show and tell a story to my classmates.

I empty the wastebasket.

My, it is windy!

The school doctor examines my throat. Ahhhh!

I write on the board.

I am a school crossing guard and I help the children to cross the road safely!

This is Me!

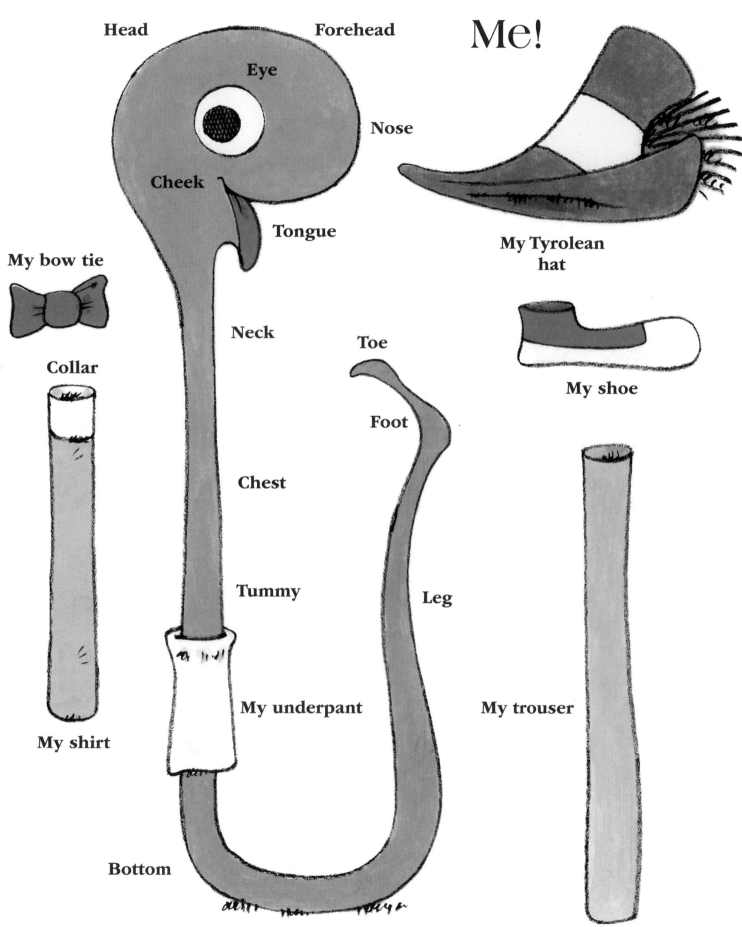

Head

Forehead

Eye

Nose

Cheek

Tongue

My Tyrolean hat

My bow tie

Neck

Toe

My shoe

Collar

Foot

Chest

Tummy

Leg

My underpant

My trouser

My shirt

Bottom

Lowly's Good Manners

Everyone should have good manners.

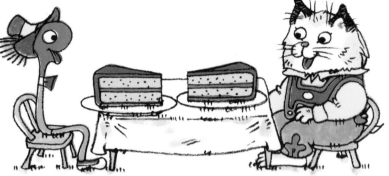

When I want something I say "Please".

When something is given to me I say "Thank you".

I hold the door open for others.

I don't interrupt when others are talking.

I help do the dishes.

I am a good helper. I help tie shoelaces.

I sit up straight at the table.
Sometimes I forget to take off my hat.

I always take
my turn.

I don't push or shove others.

I share my things.

I never fight, for that is very bad manners.

I read stories to
younger children.

When I leave after a visit to someone else's house
I always say "Thank you for a very nice time".

Counting with Lowly

I can count! You can, too!

1 One Lowly
Worm driving.

2 Two cats smiling.

3 Three pigs
crying.

4 Four dogs
singing.

5 Five foxes
sleeping.

6 Six mice honking.

honk!

honk! honk! honk! honk! honk!

7 Seven frogs swimming.

8 Eight rabbits running.

9 Nine crows crowing.

10 Ten bugs jumping!

11
Eleven hornblowers playing.

12
Twelve skiers skiing.

13
Thirteen hikers hiking.

14
Fourteen sledgers sledging.

15
Fifteen drivers driving.

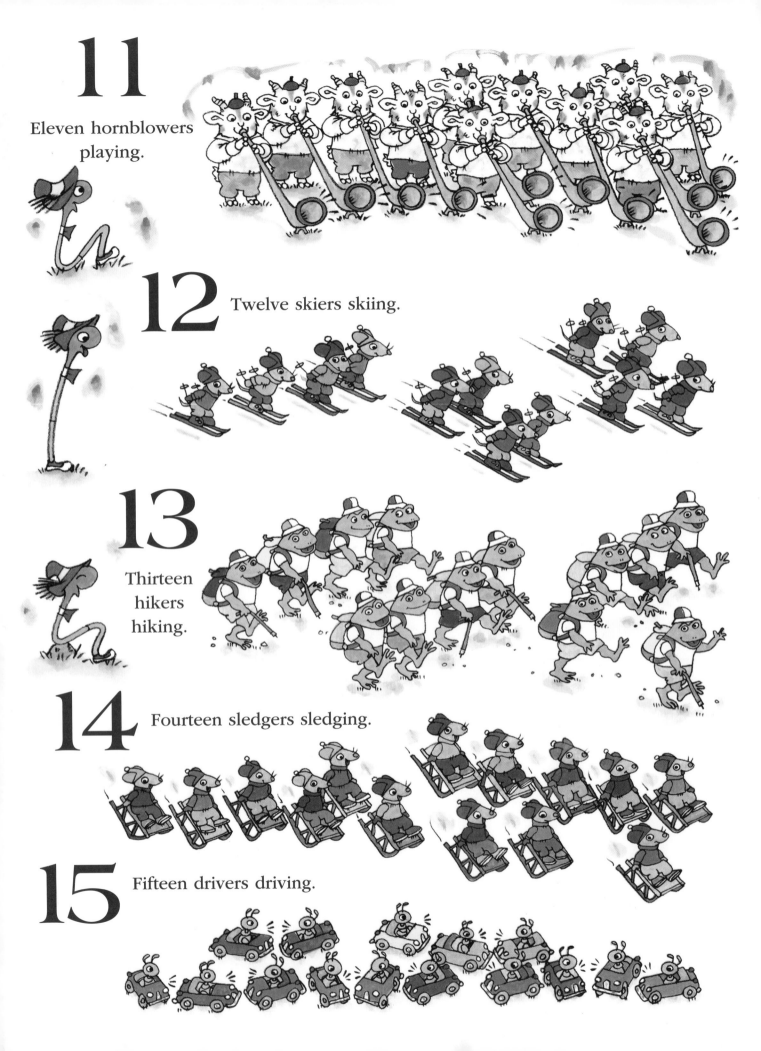

16

Sixteen toy drummers drumming.

17

Seventeen cuckoo clocks cuckooing.

18

Eighteen witches flying.

19

Nineteen socks drying.

20

Twenty chicks hatching.

peep! *peep!* *peep!*

A Visit to Farmer Pig

It is fun to visit Farmer Pig's farm.

We plough the field.

We plant the seeds.

I water the plants.

I gather the eggs from the henhouse. Sometimes I drop an egg or two. Oops! Sorry, Farmer Pig!

I pump water for Mrs. Pig.

I pick apples from the apple tree.

I help Farmer Pig to bring his apples to the market.

Meanwhile, the corn has grown tall! When the corn is ripe, we all sit down and enjoy a delicious picnic.

Hop Aboard with Lowly!

I like to take trips.

Sometimes I fly in my applecopter.

Sometimes I fly a light plane.

Other times I fly in a big jet plane.

SWISSAIR

I am always happy sailing my little sailboat.

A motorboat can go very fast over the water.

A submarine can go on top of the water or under the water.

To visit outer space I travel in a space capsule.

Sometimes I fly in my appleballoon! It's fun!

GSTAAD ♥ MY LOVE

Trains speed along the tracks from town to town and from city to city.

To get around the neighbourhood, I ride my bike!

My applecar takes me on many trips in the country.

Busy Workers on the Go

I am a busy worker. I help other busy workers do their jobs.

I help Millie the Milklady deliver her bottles of milk.

Smoky and Squirty let me ride on the fire engine!

I cruise around with Officer Simpson in the police car.

Cleaner Casey and I clean the streets.

I help Postman Pig deliver the mail.

Big Gussie and I pick up the rubbish around town.

Rikki and I drive the children to school.

Taxis drive here, there and everywhere.

I deliver eggs for Farmer Pig.
Sometimes I break one or two.
Oops! Sorry, Farmer Pig!

Things I Can Do.
Can You Do Them, Too?

These are some of the things I can do.

I can crawl.

I can hop.

I can kneel.

I can sit.

I can ride.

I can read.

I can draw.

I can also stand on my head.

I can run.

I can eat.

I can kick.

I can laugh.

I can swim.

I can talk.

Where's Lowly?

I like to play hide and seek.
Can you find me?

Am I in the attic?

In the bedroom?

In the wardrobe?

In the kitchen?

Am I in the bathroom?

On the patio?

In the basement?

At the playground?

Am I in the hall?

In the garage?

In the garden?

On the washing line?

Am I in the field?

In the apple tree?

In the frog pond?

In the workshop?

Where am I?

Good Night, Lowly!

A busy day is almost done!

Some evenings Father Cat plays
ball with us in the garden.

Then sometimes
we come in and
watch television.

We help to set the supper table.

And we tell each other
what we did today.

Then it's time for a bath!

I brush my teeth.

Afterwards, Father Cat
reads us a story.

Then it is time for bed.

Good night, everyone!
Sleep tight!

See you in
the morning!

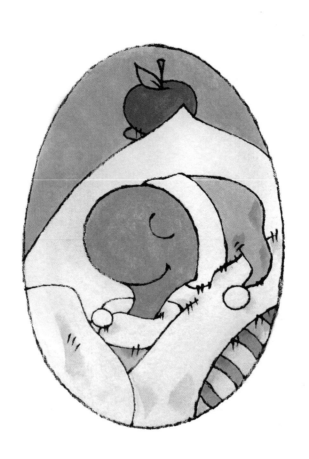